Frogwilla
A Treefrog's Story

To Maddi,
May your imagination
take you to new places!
Keri L. Hallwood

Frogwilla
A Treefrog's Story

a tale of hope,
friendship, and courage

Cheri L. Hallwood

illustrated by Aubrey M. Curl
and Harry Hallwood
inspired by Hannah P. Curl

Forever Young Publishers
Niles, Michigan

For My Granddaughters,
Ali, Aubrey, Hannah, Maisie, Abigail, and Bronwyn.

First Edition 2014

Publisher's Cataloging-in-Publication
(Provided by Quality Books, Inc.)

Hallwood, Cheri L.
Frogwilla : a treefrog's story : a tale of hope, friendship, and courage / Cheri L. Hallwood ; illustrated by Aubrey M. Curl and Harry Hallwood ; inspired by Hannah P. Curl. -- First edition
pages cm
SUMMARY: A tale about a young treefrog named Frogwilla and her quest to find her mama and papa after a late summer storm floods the banks of the great pond and separates her from her family and her home, Willow's End.
Audience: Ages 7-12.
LCCN 2014906617
ISBN 9780977442270
ISBN 9780977442263

1. Hylidae—Juvenile fiction. [1. Tree frogs—Fiction. 2. Frogs—Fiction.] I. Curl, Aubrey M., illustrator. II. Hallwood, Harry, illustrator. III. Title.

PZ7.H16553Fro 2014   [E]
                          QBI14-600078

Printed in the United States of America
McNaughton & Gunn, Inc.
960 Woodland Drive
Saline, Michigan 48176

This book was printed in Adobe Garamond Pro.
The illustrations were done in pencil.

Published by Forever Young Publishers
P.O. Box 216, Niles, Michigan 49120
visit us at www.foreveryoungpublishers.com

Contents

Frogwilla's
Journey

Willow's End

Great Pond

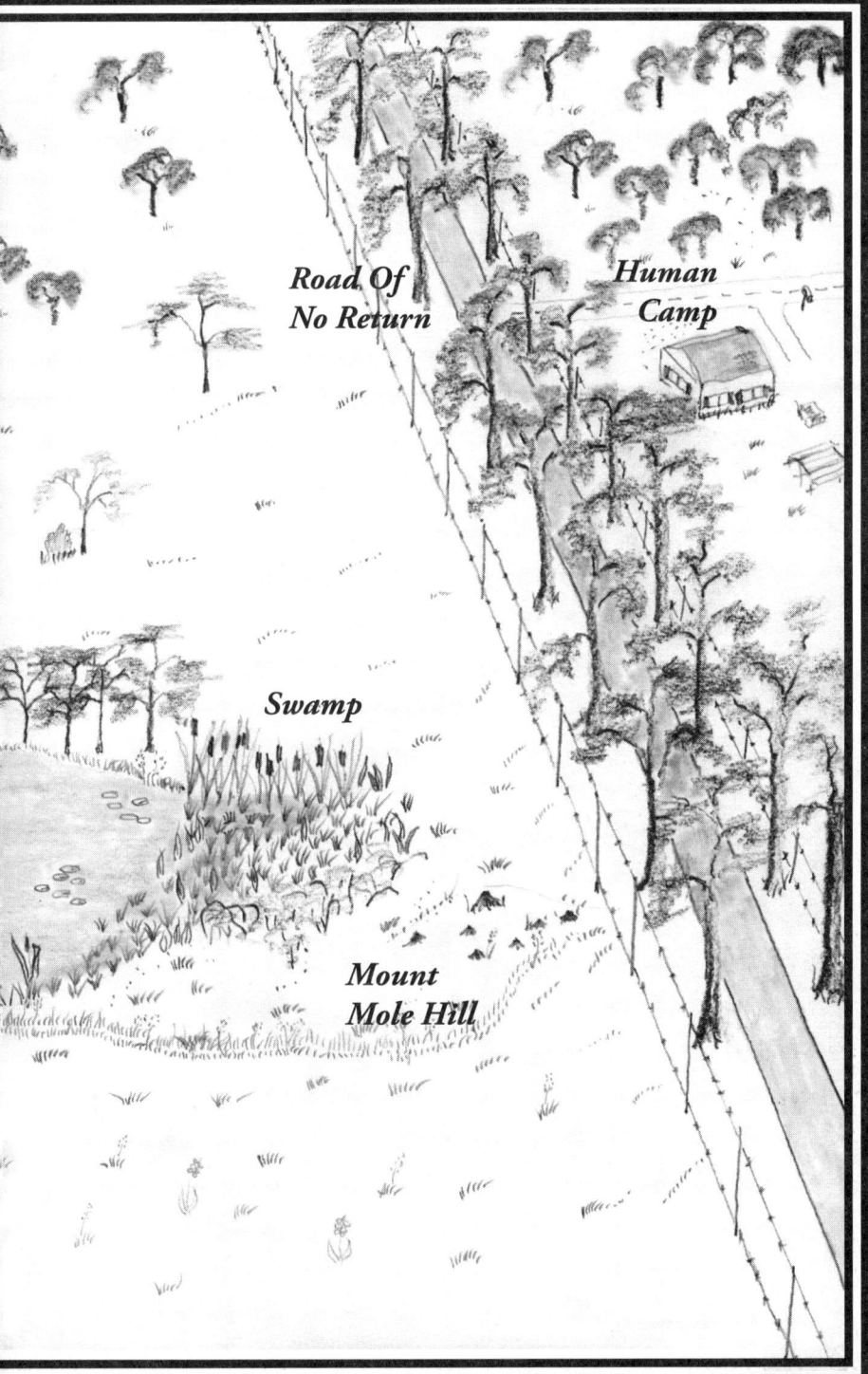

Road Of
No Return

Human
Camp

Swamp

Mount
Mole Hill

Because Hannah asked for a Chapter Book

Part One
A Midsummer's Day

Chapter One

My Home, Willow's End

I know no other way to tell my story than to start from the beginning. Not from my days as a tadpole or a froglet, but from my first summer as a young treefrog.

My story begins on the banks of a great pond, on a day that started out like most midsummer days. The air was hot and humid. A huge yellow sun had just begun to peek through some trees that lined the edge of the pond. Its shining rays filled the sky with bright shades of red and orange — casting a warm glow over the cattails and lily pads that grew at the deep end. Soon the morning mist that covered the pond's clear waters would slowly disappear. And once again, the pond would come to life with the sounds of all the living creatures that called her home. I had no way of knowing it would be a day that would change my world as I had come to know it; but, my friend, it did.

As the sun continued its morning journey, its rays soon reached the bank on the far side of the great pond. Near the top of the bank grew the most magnificent willow tree. Her long, slender branches hung like an umbrella as they stretched out toward the water's edge. And there, nestled beneath the willow's strong and twisted roots was the first place I would come to know as home, my home, Willow's End.

Because it was my first summer on the pond, there was much to learn. Mama and Papa had spent a great deal of time teaching me everything they knew about being a treefrog. You know, the

Near the top of the bank grew the most magnificent willow tree.

usual treefrog stuff. Like how to catch bugs, how to avoid my enemies, how to leap the farthest, and, oh yes, how to climb trees and shrubs . . . what treefrogs do best.

My parents knew how much I wanted to learn these skills. I tried my very best to do everything just as I was taught. But some things were more challenging than others, especially tree climbing.

Mama would tell Papa that climbing was a bit more difficult for me because of my size. You see, I was quite small, even for a treefrog. Papa would just nod his head and smile. He knew that Mama was very protective of me. And every now and then he would remind me that Mama had good reason to be this way.

I remember hearing Papa's stories about how he and Mama had longed to be parents. But for many springs they had watched helplessly as Mama's tiny tadpoles became victims to the many fish that lived in the pond. Not one tadpole had survived, that was, until me.

It would be no different on this summer

morning. Even before my eyes had time to get used to the morning light, I heard my mama's sweet voice, her special trill, as she called to me like she did every morning.

"Good morning, my little Frogwilla," Mama said with a loving smile, as she nudged me with her cool, wet nose. "It's time to rise and shine! Time to leap and climb! Young treefrogs must learn all they can while the days are warm and long. Before you know it the days in Willow's End will grow short and the air will turn cold. Then it will be time for us to sleep until next spring."

"Yeeess, Mama," I replied with a long sigh.

From out of the corner of my eye, I could see Papa grin as he hopped up next to Mama and gave her a loving nudge.

"Now, now, my love," Mama said blushing, "not in front of Frogwilla." Mama always turned bright green when she blushed. And she always blushed when Papa showed his affection for her while I was watching.

"Your mama knows what's best!" Papa agreed.

"It's important for you to learn something new every day, to be the best you can be. After all, Frogwilla, someday you will be all grown-up and have young treefrogs of your own."

While I lay there listening to Papa's words of advice, I began to daydream. I tried to imagine being all grown-up with young treefrogs of my own. But most of all, I thought about being on my own, without him or Mama. I couldn't even begin to think of such a thing.

As my thoughts began to fade, I suddenly heard Papa call out my name.

"Frogwilla! Frogwilla, did you hear what I just said?" I could tell by the tone of his voice that something was wrong.

"No, Papa!" I answered, trying to gather my thoughts.

"We have no time to waste!" shouted Papa. "I smell rain in the air. We must start your lessons now before the weather changes, before the rains come. I feel a storm is brewing."

I had been so caught up in my daydreaming that

I failed to notice how the sun's rays were no longer peeking through the branches of the willow tree. The morning sky, with its bright shades of red and orange, was now filled with dark, gray clouds.

A strange stillness had suddenly silenced the voices of every living thing on the great pond.

It was then I noticed that the grin on Papa's face had quickly changed to a look of great concern. Even Mama had a worried look on her face.

No one would be prepared for what was about to happen on that beautiful summer's day, especially me.

My name is Frogwilla, and this is my story.

Chapter Two
Lessons to Learn

"Hurry, my little Frogwilla!" Papa called out, as he watched the gray clouds continue to gather over our heads. "There is no time to dilly-dally. Mama and I have another busy day planned for you. We must get started with your morning lesson, before the storm hits."

The familiar nest of cool, wet willow leaves I had swaddled around me felt so lovely. Oh, how I loved spending long, lazy mornings in my nest beneath the willow.

I remember thinking, *storm or no storm, I was*

not about to leave my comfy nest! After all, I never was an early riser. Besides, I was sure I knew what Mama and Papa had planned for me that day. It was sure to be another day of practicing my tree climbing skills. Something I was not looking forward to at all!

My parents each had their own special skills, and they had gone to great lengths to make sure I would learn them.

Papa had spent many days teaching me how to avoid my enemies, like skunks, raccoons, and snakes. This was not my favorite skill to learn, because I found this very scary.

Mama had done her very best to teach me how to catch the most tasty bugs with my long, sticky tongue. This was my favorite skill to learn, because I loved to eat.

But most importantly, they both had spent many, many days trying their very best to teach me how to use my unique, sticky toe pads to climb and cling to the branches of trees . . . what all treefrogs do best. All, that is, except me.

You see, it hadn't taken me very long to discover I didn't really like climbing. Every time I tried to climb, even a few frog-lengths up a young sapling or a small cattail, I would freeze with fear. My heart would begin to beat faster and faster. My toe pads would sweat so badly that I would lose my grip and slide down whatever I was attempting to climb.

During one of my many practice days, I remember overhearing Mama whisper to Papa that she was sure I was afraid of heights. "Nonsense!" had been Papa's only reply.

"Come along, Frogwilla," called Mama. "Your papa is starting to pace the ground. We must quickly get started with today's lessons!"

I could hear bumblebees and butterflies as they flew around Willow's End. I was sure they must be waiting to see if today might be the day I would finally cling to something that was taller than me. Most everyone that lived in or around the great pond had heard of my lack of tree climbing skills.

But Mama always said, *"From out of small acts of*

courage come great rewards." I knew that someday I would have the courage to face my fear of climbing. I just knew it wasn't going to be today.

As Papa hopped back and forth in front of Mama, I could see he was becoming impatient.

"Coming, Papa," I said, as I started to brush aside the lovely cool leaves nestled beneath me. I yawned and then took one more long stretch before finally wiggling out of my comfy nest.

"Come along, Frogwilla," said Mama. "We'll start your climbing lesson today with a young seedling."

"Now, now, my dear," interrupted Papa. "This isn't her first climbing lesson, you know! Frogwilla needs to challenge herself, to try a little harder. I think we will start off with a more mature tree, maybe something a little taller."

I could tell Mama wasn't very happy with Papa's choice of words, or trees. She smiled and nodded. Not her usual happy smile. It was the kind of smile Mama used when she did not approve of something.

"I think I will hop over and visit the meadow while you two continue with Frogwilla's lesson," said Mama.

"Why of course, my dear," replied Papa. "But please don't be too long. This storm that's brewing seems to be rolling in lickety-split!"

After giving me one of her gentle, loving nose rubs, Mama disappeared, as she leaped into the tall grasses that lined the edge of the pond leading up to the meadow.

I knew this was Mama's way of trying her best to show Papa and me she was not being over-protective. But secretly I knew Mama would be somewhere close by — hiding and watching over me like she always did.

As I watched her leave, I took a deep breath, swallowed hard, and turned to join Papa for my climbing lesson.

But secretly I knew Mama would be somewhere close by — hiding and watching over me like she always did.

Chapter Three

A Storm Brews

The dark, gray clouds that Papa had been watching were now changing to strange and unusual shades of green and black.

I remember hoping the rains would come soon so that my climbing lesson would have to wait until tomorrow. I was sure that any day but today would be a better day for climbing. But alas, my lesson began!

Sometimes Papa would start the day's lesson with a little game of hide-and-go-leap. Mama said this was Papa's way of helping me build my climbing skills. She said it had to do with something called "confidence."

"How about a game of hide-and-go-leap today?" asked Papa, as he smiled and winked at me.

"Of course, Papa," I replied. "I was hoping you'd ask."

Papa was the best climber. And he was really good at playing games, especially hide-and-go-leap. Papa took great pride in how he could change the color of his skin. If we played in the long meadow grasses, he would be green. But if we played on fallen tree limbs, he would turn gray. I, on the other hand, was only able to be green right now.

"That's not fair!" I always complained. "You're too hard to find, Papa!"

"Now, now, Frogwilla!" Papa would say. "Someday soon you will be able to change your color, just like Mama and me. Maybe by next summer."

After our game, he'd grin and lift me up onto

his strong back and treat me to a froggy-back ride. Oh, how I loved those froggy-back rides!

But that morning my froggy-back ride was cut short. And my climbing lesson didn't happen. Without warning, the strange colored clouds began to swirl around with a force of wind like I had never seen or felt before.

"We must move quickly," Papa said. "It looks like today's climbing lesson will have to wait. I think this is going to be much more than a summer storm. The air smells different. Something is not right. I must go and find your mama. We must return to Willow's End."

"But Papa, we haven't even . . . ," I started to say.

The look on Papa's face made me realize something was truly wrong. This was not the time to question anything he might say or do. But secretly, I was very relieved not to have to climb that day.

I watched as Papa began to hop around and around in circles, searching for Mama.

"Frogwilla, stay right here. Don't go anywhere!" Papa said in a firm voice. "I'll be back for you as soon as I find your mama. She must have gone back to Willow's End."

Without saying another word, he leaped into the thick undergrowth that grew along the banks of the pond.

I felt so scared! I had never been left alone before. *What if Mama and Papa couldn't find their way back to me? Who would take care of me? Would I ever learn to climb?*

As I impatiently waited for their return, the rain began to fall. And it fell hard! It fell so hard and fast it felt like small pebbles as it hit my body, not like a gentle summer's rain. I could no longer see even one frog-length in front of me. *What should I do? Should I stay, like Papa said? Or should I try to go home, back to Willow's End?*

Suddenly, from behind the tall cattails, I saw something heading my way. The rapidly falling rain made it difficult to see what the something was. But whatever it was, it was definitely heading full speed straight for me!

Before I could even blink an eye, I heard the something call out my name.

"Frogwilla! Frogwilla!" a familiar voice shouted. "Where are you, Frogwilla?"

The *something* was my mama!

"I'm right here, Mama!" I answered with great relief.

Yes, Mama had found me! And I could see Papa following close behind her.

I remember hearing the fright in Mama's voice as she called out to Papa, "Hurry, my love, hurry! We must all get back to Willow's End before the wind carries us away."

"Yes, Papa, hurry!" I cried out.

But Papa didn't answer. When I turned around, I saw he was gone. *Where was he? He was there just a moment ago. Had the wind truly carried him far, far away?*

Mama knew she had to act quickly. There was no time to waste. She called out to Papa one more time. Still there was no answer. Mama had no choice; we needed to find our way back home. Staying close beside me, she safely led the way through the whirling wind and rushing rain.

As soon as Mama and I reached Willow's End, she used her strong nose to push me safely between the large roots of the mighty willow tree.

Mama and I held onto each other tightly as we huddled beneath the willow. The wind howled! The rain beat rapidly into the ground! We watched as the pond's waters began to rise. Mama and I now feared the worst for Papa.

Then, just as the water was about to reach our nest, Papa appeared! He had somehow managed to find his way back to us, back to Willow's End. I cannot begin to tell you what a wonderful feeling it was to see my papa. We were all together again, safe and out of the storm.

But when Papa lifted his head, I saw that the look on his face had changed once again. He tried not to show it, to be brave for both Mama and me. Yet, somehow, I knew he was scared — just like me!

*Then, just as the water was about to
reach our nest, Papa appeared!*

The next words that Papa said were the most terrifying words I would ever hear . . . *"We must climb!"*

Chapter Four
The Storm

As I lay huddled next to Mama, I soon began to shake and tremble. Not from the cold rain, but from the words that Papa had just said. I saw by the look on Mama's face that she understood what must be done. There was no time to waste.

"Frogwilla, please hurry," Papa called out, as he led the way up the willow tree.

We all watched in disbelief as the pouring rain rushed up the banks of the great pond and headed straight for our nest — straight for Willow's End. The water was now rising so quickly we barely had time to think.

"Stay close to your mama!" Papa said. "Don't look down! We must climb as high as we can to escape the force of the rising water."

I could see Mama was trying her very best to remain calm and not show her fear. She was not afraid for herself; Mama was afraid for me, knowing how afraid I was to climb.

"But Frogwilla hasn't . . . ," Mama started to say, as she held me close to her side.

"No time to worry, my dear," Papa replied. "We must not look back. Everyone stay close and follow me!"

I could see that Papa was doing his best to keep everyone calm and together.

And then it happened!

Suddenly, without warning, the power of the rapidly moving water engulfed us, sweeping us all out toward the deep end of the pond — separating me from both Mama and Papa.

"Mama, Papa!" I shouted, as I struggled to keep my head above the water.

It wasn't long before I saw they had become trapped between some broken tree limbs and were now being pulled downstream by the flood's strong waters. Papa soon managed to free himself. But the tug from the current was too strong for him. It quickly pulled him under and soon my papa disappeared from sight.

I could hear Mama, off in the distance, as she called out to Papa and me.

"Stay together! I'll find you both!" she called out again and again. "Be brave, Frogwilla! Be brave, my little one!"

Helplessly, I watched as Mama drifted farther and farther away, far beyond the boundaries of the great pond and Willow's End. But I knew Mama was a strong swimmer. She would find us. I was certain she would.

I did my best to swim with the current, just like Mama had taught me, but the water's strength was more than I could handle. I fought hard to keep my head above the rising water, trying desperately to find something to cling to.

It all happened so fast. Just when I was certain I was going to be swallowed up by the angry water, I felt something grab hold of me and lift me from the water's clutches.

"I've gotcha!" Papa yelled.

I took a long, deep breath as he lifted me out of the water and onto an empty bottle floating beside me.

"Papa, Papa! It's you!" I cried out with joy.

"Hold on tight, Frogwilla! This should keep us afloat and help us ride out the flood water to safer ground."

With my arms safely wrapped around Papa, I began to tell him what had happened to Mama. I told him how she said we must stay together and that she'd find us. We both agreed Mama was a strong swimmer and that one way or another we would be together again.

I don't know how long we stayed afloat. And I don't know how long it was before I realized both Papa and I were beginning to tire. I only know it wasn't long before Papa noticed that the bottle was beginning to fill up with water.

Papa looked me straight in the eye and with a loving smile said, "Frogwilla, once again you must be brave. You must do what I say. You must jump to the nearest tree and climb. Soon this will be filled with water, and it will sink."

"But Papa, I can't leave you," I said. "I won't leave you! Mama said to stay together." But I could see Papa was now too weak to swim or even leap to safety. I knew I must obey.

The next moment, I found myself leaping high above the water. Up, up, toward the sky, like a fledgling flying from its mama's nest.

I don't remember exactly how I got there. I only remember waking up and finding myself clinging to the top branch of a small tree. There I was, high above the waters the storm had left behind.

It wasn't long before the strong winds and heavy rains stopped. The storm had left just as suddenly as it had arrived. It was almost as if nothing had ever happened, like it was a dream or something.

*The next moment, I found myself
leaping high above the water.*

But, my friend, it was not a dream. I was awake, and I was alone.

Chapter Five
Alone

From high atop my safe perch in the tree, for as far as I could see was water . . . lots and lots of water. It seemed to have no beginning, no end. The great pond that had once been a big part of my home seemed to have completely disappeared. It was as if it had been swallowed up by the storm. The tall trees and meadow grasses that once graced her banks had now been replaced with deep and murky water. It was a kind of water like I had never seen before. I could see no cattails, no lily pads, no Willow's End . . . No Mama, No Papa!

As the sun began to set on that fateful summer's day, my thoughts were only of my mama and papa. I felt so sad and so alone. I kept asking myself the same questions over and over, again and again . . . *Where had the water taken them? What if they were hurt? When would we be together again?*

I cannot say how long I waited, or what time of the night it was before I finally fell asleep. But as I slept on my perch high above the water, I soon began to dream. My dreams took me back to Willow's End, and to thoughts of Mama and Papa. I dreamed about tomorrow and about how I would do whatever I needed to do and go wherever I needed to go to find them. And as I dreamed about tomorrow, I could hear my mama's sweet trill calling out to me . . .

"Be brave, my little one.
For out of small acts of courage
Come great rewards."

Suddenly, I awoke from my dream to find

myself slipping down the tree branch, straight down toward the deep water. Quickly, without even thinking, I found myself using all my toes to grab hold of the tree and return to my safe perch. It was only then I realized that I, Frogwilla, had actually climbed up a tree! Yes, somehow I had found the courage to jump and cling with my sticky toes. Just like Mama and Papa said I would. *If only they could see me now,* I thought. *They would be so proud!*

As I gazed out into the night sky, I slowly drifted back to sleep. And once again, I found myself dreaming about tomorrow. Yes, tomorrow would be a new day, a new beginning. It would be the beginning of my journey, my quest to find my mama and papa.

Part Two
My Journey Begins

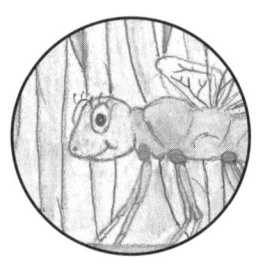

Chapter Six
Sunshine

When I awoke the next morning, the air was very still. Warm rays of sunlight peeked through the early morning clouds. The only sounds I heard were those of birds chirping and bees buzzing as they flew past me.

While I sat on my safe perch, I soon began to daydream about flying. I could only imagine how wonderful that might be, especially now.

When I turned and looked down from my tree branch, I saw that although the current had slowed down to an easy flow, the water was still murky and very high. I was certain it was not safe for me to begin my search for Mama and Papa. As much as it saddened me, I knew I would need to stay on my safe branch and patiently wait for the water to go down . . . and so I waited!

I have no idea how much time passed before the storm's waters finally lowered enough for me to begin my climb down, but it must have been a long time. I was now beginning to feel very hungry.

You can imagine my surprise when I looked down and discovered that my branch was not part of a *small* tree. It was actually one of the top branches of a very *tall* tree. As I looked down at the ground below, my heart began to pound and my toes began to sweat. I could see it was a long, long way down!

"Oh no, not again," I said to myself. "This can't be happening to me. I must get down from here. Come on toes, don't fail me now! Frogwilla, you can do this! After all, you are a treefrog."

Once again, my thoughts were of Mama and her

words, *"Be brave, my little one!"* So I took a deep breath, wiggled my toes and slowly, very slowly began my downward climb.

"I did it!" I shouted out loud, as I landed rather clumsily on some muddy moss beneath the tree.

Upon my not-so-graceful landing, I soon noticed that it wasn't just the moss that was muddy, it was muddy everywhere! Everything, for as far as I could see, was covered with this brown, sticky, smelly mud. As I looked around me, I saw many pieces of fallen trees and jagged rocks peeking through the mud. I was sure getting through or around this mess wasn't going to be easy. But despite my not-so-great climbing skills, I was quite confident in my jumping skills.

As I leaped my way from rock to rock, I began to hear and feel this rumbling noise coming from my tummy. I soon realized I must find something to eat before going any further.

After enjoying a delicious meal of grubs and other goodies that the flood waters had left behind, I found myself beginning to tire. I was about to leap over to another rock, when something caught my eye. There, just beyond the mud, was a small, grassy patch of ground and on it grew one lovely wildflower. Maybe, just maybe, this flower would be the perfect place for me to rest for a while.

It took only a few long leaps over the thick, smelly mud before I reached the wildflower. To my delight, it looked like the perfect place to rest. Not too high, not too small, and no mud. . . . it was just right! So I hopped inside.

I had barely begun to close my eyes, when I saw something whiz past me. There was a bright flash of color followed by a big gust of wind. It almost took my breath away. As I quickly opened my eyes, I found myself face to face with one of the fastest and most amazing flying creatures I had ever seen! It had six legs just like bumblebees and fireflies, but its body and wings were much larger. Its see-through wings seemed to sparkle, as it magically hovered in front of me.

"Hello, there!" said the flying creature, as it gently landed on one of the flower's large leaves.

*"Hello, there!" said the flying creature, as it gently
landed on one of the flower's large leaves.*

I was so frightened that I did not know what to say or do. It was as if my body was frozen. I only hoped it hadn't noticed how frightened I really was. I remember thinking that if I stayed very still it might not see me.

"I said HELLO! Did you not hear me?" It repeated with a puzzled look. "Something got your tongue?"

"No!" I replied, as I looked up and puffed out my chest. (Papa always said that if I puffed out my chest it would make me look bigger and feel braver.) "Just *who* and *what* are you?"

"My name is Sunshine," answered the creature. "I'm the fastest dragonfly around! What's your name? You look like some kind of frog."

Before I could find the courage to answer her, Sunshine darted off and began to fly in circles around me. She was amazingly fast! Then, in the blink of an eye, she was back standing on the large leaf in front of me.

"My name is Frogwilla," I quickly answered, before Sunshine had time to dart off again. "I'm a treefrog."

"Hmmm," said Sunshine, looking even more puzzled than before. "A treefrog, you say? You sure are awfully small for a frog."

Then, before I could reply, she said, "Silly me. Why, of course, you're one of those tree-huggers! I've heard about you. Are you lost?"

"No, I don't think so," I answered. "I just don't know where I am. And I'm alone."

"Oh, so you're an orphan — like me!" Sunshine replied.

"What's an *orphan?*" I asked.

"It's when someone doesn't have a mama and papa," explained Sunshine. She went on to tell me she never knew her parents and how, at an early age, she became part of a family of other dragonflies that were also orphans.

"But I'm *not* an orphan!" I shouted. "I know who my parents are. And I am *not* lost! I am off to find them."

Now, for the first time since we met, Sunshine sat very still and listened quietly as I began to tell her all about Willow's End and the terrible storm that had separated me from my mama and papa.

Before I knew what was happening, Sunshine began flying rapidly in circles around me. She swooped over my head as if she were going to pick me up and carry me off somewhere.

"I know," Sunshine proudly announced, as she hovered over me. "I have a brilliant idea! I will help you find your mama and papa. After all, I am the fastest dragonfly around! And I know a lot about the meadows, swamps, and woods. What do you say to that, little Frogwilla?"

Once again, I found myself speechless. To think that a dragonfly like Sunshine would be so kind as to offer to help me look for my parents, I truly did not know what to say. So I simply smiled and nodded *YES!*

"Well then," exclaimed Sunshine, "let's get hopping! Soon it will be dark."

And so, with the help of the fastest dragonfly around, my journey began.

Chapter Seven
Tucker

As I looked up toward the sky, I could see that Sunshine was correct. The daylight was now fading, and the moon had begun to faintly show itself for the first time in many days.

"Come along now," Sunshine called, as she began to fly overhead. Then, looking a bit confused, she suddenly paused and hovered in midair.

"Oh, silly me," exclaimed Sunshine, as she landed beside me. "I forgot to ask which way do we go. I mean, do we head out toward where the sun goes down or where the sun comes up? One must always have a plan, you know."

"Well," I answered, trying to gather my thoughts. "The last time I saw either one of my parents the sun had not been out at all. So I'm not sure which way to go."

As we stood there staring at each other, it finally came to me. I remembered that when I woke up the morning after the storm, I had seen the sun come up in the direction of where I had last seen my mama and papa drift away.

"This way," I shouted with confidence, as I pointed directly to my right. "Follow me!"

Sunshine smiled, for now we had a plan.

We hadn't traveled very far or for very long before I discovered that, plan or no plan, Sunshine did not like traveling once it became dark. She said it had something to do with her eyesight. We agreed to find a place to bed down for the night. After all, we both could use a good night's sleep.

I soon found some dry, crumpled-up leaves lying beneath a dead tree stump and snuggled up among them. Sunshine continued to dart about in her usual manner before finally settling down atop the tree stump above me.

That night we learned a lot about each other. Sunshine told me all about the marsh where she lived and how long she had been on her own before joining the other dragonflies. She also took great pleasure in telling me that not only was she the fastest dragonfly around, but that she could fly backwards just as fast as she could fly forward. I was impressed!

When it was my turn, I told Sunshine all about the great pond and Willow's End. I told her that when I got older, I would be able to change my skin color from green to gray, just like my mama and papa. I could tell she was impressed!

It wasn't long before we both fell fast asleep.

The next morning, I awoke to find that Sunshine was gone. As I hopped from beneath the tree stump, I couldn't help but wonder why my new-found friend would just fly off and leave me. You can imagine my relief when I suddenly heard the familiar sound of Sunshine's wings as she whizzed over my head and landed back atop the tree stump.

"Good morning, sleepyhead!" smiled Sunshine. "I've been up since daylight. Been out and about asking everyone I know if they had seen any treefrogs traveling around together. Or if any kind of frogs looked like they might be looking for something or someone. I even told them about your mama's special call, her trill. Then a little butterfly approached me and suggested I fly over to a place called Mount Mole Hill. She said someone there might be able to help us."

I had been so focused on listening to everything Sunshine was telling me that I hadn't even noticed there was something moving in the grasses right behind me.

"I heard you might be looking for some treefrogs!" said the *something*, as it suddenly touched me from behind with its very cold nose.

Startled, I quickly leaped into the air, almost knocking down Sunshine, who was trying her best to get out of my way.

"Why, look," declared Sunshine, as she steadied herself in midair. "It's a turtle. Haven't you ever seen a turtle before, Frogwilla?"

While I slowly shook my head *no*, I bent down to take a look at the strange creature standing below me. Whatever it was, it looked as if it was stuck inside some kind of large, bumpy rock. The only parts sticking out from the rock were its head, four legs, and a short tail. *Could this turtle possibly know something about my parents?*

"What's your name, little turtle?" Sunshine asked.

"My name is Tucker," answered the turtle, in a slow, clear voice. "I heard that a dragonfly was flying around asking about some treefrogs. Would either one of you know anything about this?"

"Yes! Yes!" I quickly answered. "That would be me . . . I mean us. Have you seen my mama and papa? Do you know where they might be?"

Tucker went on to tell us how he had seen a pair of treefrogs just a few days ago, right after the terrible storm. He told us how he watched as the

*"Why look," declared Sunshine,
as she steadied herself in midair. "It's a turtle."*

storm's waters carried them past him.

"I didn't really think too much about it," Tucker said, stretching out his long wrinkly neck. "They just looked like so many of the other frogs the storm had left behind. But I do remember one thing. There was something special about the sound coming from one of the treefrogs. It reminded me of the call of a songbird. It sounded like it was calling out a name: Frogzilla or Bogwilla."

I couldn't hold back my excitement any longer. I shouted out loud and strong, "Frogwilla! Mama was calling my name, Frogwilla! That's me! Can you please take me to my mama and papa? Please, Tucker, please."

Tucker said he wasn't sure if the pair of frogs he had seen really were my parents, but I had no doubts. I was sure! So he quickly agreed to take Sunshine and me to the place where he had last seen them.

"Follow me," said Tucker. "It's just beyond Mount Mole Hill."

"Mount Mole Hill!" I exclaimed. "Sunshine

told me that a butterfly said someone there might be able to help me find my parents."

"Maybe, maybe not," Tucker replied. "But it won't be easy getting to Mount Mole Hill. There's only one way to get there. We must travel along the edge of a swamp where an army of giant bullfrogs is said to roam."

Chapter Eight
Sarge

"Well now," said Sunshine, as she impatiently hovered in front of Tucker. "Before we head for this Mount Mole Hill, shouldn't you tell us more about the swamp and these bullyfrogs?"

Tucker held his head low as he slowly turned around to face both Sunshine and me. I remember how nervous Tucker appeared to be as he started to speak.

"First of all, they are *bullfrogs*, not bullyfrogs," whispered Tucker, carefully looking to see if anyone else might be listening. "And from what I've heard from others who have wandered anywhere near the swamp, these frogs are big, and they are mean!"

Sunshine and I were now spellbound and more curious than ever!

"The story goes," Tucker began, "that at one time these bullfrogs were kind and friendly. They used to help other creatures travel through the dark and dangerous waters of the swamp. But then humans came into the swamp and began to hunt them down."

Tucker paused for a moment, once again checking to make sure we were alone.

"Go ahead," I whispered, looking over my shoulder. "Tell us more."

With a fearful look in his eyes, Tucker went on with the story. He told us how the humans would hide in the swamp grass and wait for the bullfrogs. Then, when one of the bullfrogs got close enough . . . BAM! The humans would spear him with this long, sharp stick then pick him up and throw him into a box called a cage.

"It is said," Tucker continued, "that those that

are caught are never to be seen nor heard of again. Some say that the humans keep them as prisoners. Some say they use them to play some sort of jumping game. Others say the humans actually *eat* them!"

As I sat there listening to Tucker, my thoughts drifted back to Willow's End. Up until that moment, I hadn't known much about humans, only that they were tall creatures that walked upright on two legs. The only time I had ever actually seen one was during one of my climbing lessons. It was standing near the edge of the pond holding onto a very long stick with a string dangling in the water. I remember wanting to take a closer look, but Papa said it was best for us to avoid humans.

Tucker reminded us it was getting late. He thought it best if we made it to the swamp before the sun went down.

It must have been nearly dusk before we finally reached the edge of the swamp. It was just as Tucker had described. The swamp was thick with mud. Its waters were dark and smelly. There were strange and unfamiliar sounds all around us. I remember thinking this would not be a place I would want to call home.

It wasn't long before we came upon a field of tall pointy grasses that bordered the swamp. We were just about to take a rest when I felt the ground shake beneath my legs. Suddenly, I heard this deep gravelly voice shout out from behind us.

"Intruder! Intruder!" It bellowed out. "Halt! Who goes there? Go no further or I, Sarge, Leader of the Bullfrogs, will have all of you for my dinner!"

Slowly, we all turned around. I looked up to find myself staring into the eyes of the biggest frog I had ever seen in my life. He was *gigantic!* He had large, muscular legs that reminded me of the roots of the mighty willow tree. His toes were as long as my whole body. His large, bulging eyes almost seemed to hypnotize me. He had a mouth so big and wide, it stretched from one side of his head to the other . . . big enough to swallow all three of us with just one gulp. There was no doubt in my mind — this must be one of them. This must be

*I looked up to find myself staring into
the eyes of the biggest frog I had ever seen in my life.*

a *bullfrog!*

"I am Frogwilla," I answered, struggling to find my voice. "I am here with my friends, Sunshine and Tucker. We are traveling through the swamp on our way to find my mama and papa. Maybe you might have seen them?"

At first there was only silence. It was so quiet you could have heard a dried up willow leaf fall to the ground.

Then, with the strength from his huge back legs, Sarge lunged forward. His mouth opened wide and his long, slimy tongue began to lick his lips. My heart began to pound as I felt his hot breath on my face. I was sure I was about to become his dinner.

Suddenly, from out of nowhere, I heard something zoom directly over my head. I ducked just in time to see this long, pointy stick strike Sarge in one of his back legs. He screamed out in pain as it pinned him to the ground.

Immediately I turned to see two humans come running out of the tall swamp grass and scoop up the wounded bullfrog with what looked like a bag made of strings.

Sunshine and I quickly took cover among the swamp's thick undergrowth, while Tucker retreated inside his shell. I held my breath and watched helplessly as one of the humans pulled out the stick and tossed Sarge into some box-like cage he had been carrying.

Then, from far off in the distance, came another cry of pain. Quietly, I watched as the humans raced off in the direction of the cry, leaving the box unguarded with its wounded prisoner inside.

"B-b-boy, that was close!" stuttered Tucker, as he slowly came out of the safety of his shell. "Can you believe that? The humans saved our lives from that big bad bullfrog! Hurry, let's get out of here before they return!"

It was then that I heard cries of pain coming from the once fierce bullfrog. His eyes filled with tears as he tried to use his wounded leg to escape from the cage. It was a sound I would never forget.

"But what about Sarge?" I asked. "What if the

humans keep him a prisoner forever and ever, like Tucker said? Or worse yet, what if they really do *eat* him? We must try to do something to help set him free. And besides, he is a frog, just like me, only bigger."

As I turned to face Sunshine, I saw she was nodding her head in agreement with me — even though she, too, could have been eaten.

After a brief moment of silence, Sunshine spoke. "Well, it's true that we could have been the bullfrog's dinner," Sunshine admitted, as she flew around Tucker. "But I think what Frogwilla said is also true. It seems to me we have a choice to make here. We can either continue on our journey to Mount Mole Hill and forget about the bullfrog, or we can see if there is anything we can do to free him. I say we take a vote!"

I didn't know what a *vote* was, but I figured it had something to do with making a choice, like Sunshine had just said. And so we voted. One nod of a head for *no*, two nods for *yes*. The vote was two to one in favor of trying to help free Sarge.

Despite Tucker's disapproval, the decision was made. We would do our best to try to help Sarge. And we needed to do it quickly, before the humans returned.

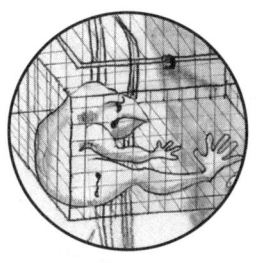

Chapter Nine
A Frog is a Frog

If we were going to try to free this bullfrog, we definitely needed a plan.

"I know!" exclaimed Sunshine, as she twirled around high above our heads. "I'll fly off and scout the area and make sure the humans are nowhere in sight. Then, when it's safe for you and Tucker to approach the cage, I'll signal you by hovering over it."

"Then what?" asked Tucker, as he slowly paced the ground.

Silently, we all looked at each other for an

answer. That's when this crazy idea came to me. I, Frogwilla, had a plan!

Maybe, just maybe, I could climb to the top of the cage, find the opening and set the bullfrog free. After all, I was both strong enough to climb and small enough to slip between the bars of the cage. Now, all I had to do was find the courage to do it!

I quickly turned to Sunshine and Tucker and began to explain my plan. They both agreed it was definitely worth a try.

Suddenly, the wounded Sarge made the most horrible sound. His voice began to vibrate with the deepest croak I had ever heard any frog make. From out of the corner of my eye, I watched as his already huge chest grew to twice its size. Again and again, he puffed out his chest, each time bellowing out the same horrible, hoarse cry. Finally, after what seemed like a very long time, he stopped, cleared his throat, and began to speak.

"Don't waste your time," croaked Sarge. "Whatever makes any of you think you can possibly help me? You are all so small and *way* too young to know much about anything. You are useless to me. Leave me!"

I turned around to see Sarge, with his body pushed tightly up against the bars of the cage, licking his wounded leg. His eyes no longer wet with tears, he now tried his best to look big and mean once again.

"Well . . . ," I started to say, only to be interrupted by the captured bullfrog.

"And furthermore, why would you want to help me? I was just about to have you for my dinner."

I don't know how I managed to find the courage to speak, but I did. I hopped right over to that cage and looked him straight in the eye and continued. "Well . . . my mama always says size doesn't matter. She says it's not how others see you on the outside, it's how you see yourself on the inside that matters. And, after all, we are *both* frogs. And I think frogs should help look out for one another, no matter what kind of frog they are. Maybe someday you, too, will help someone in trouble."

"There was a time . . . ," Sarge began.

But before he could say another word, I felt Tucker give me a hard nudge from behind. I glanced up to see Sunshine buzzing all around us like a whirlwind. I knew something was terribly wrong.

"They're coming back!" Sunshine cried out. "I can see them. The humans are coming back! Hurry, Frogwilla! Hurry! I see a small door on the top of the cage. Climb up and get inside. See if you can find the latch that's holding it down."

When I turned toward the cage, I noticed that Tucker had moved himself up next to one of the sides of the cage.

"Hop on my shell," insisted Tucker. "That will put you closer to the top of the cage. Then you won't have so far to climb. You can do it! We know you can!"

Without another word or thought, I took a deep breath, closed my eyes and leaped with all my might.

But it was too late. The human had suddenly returned and snatched up the cage, carrying it

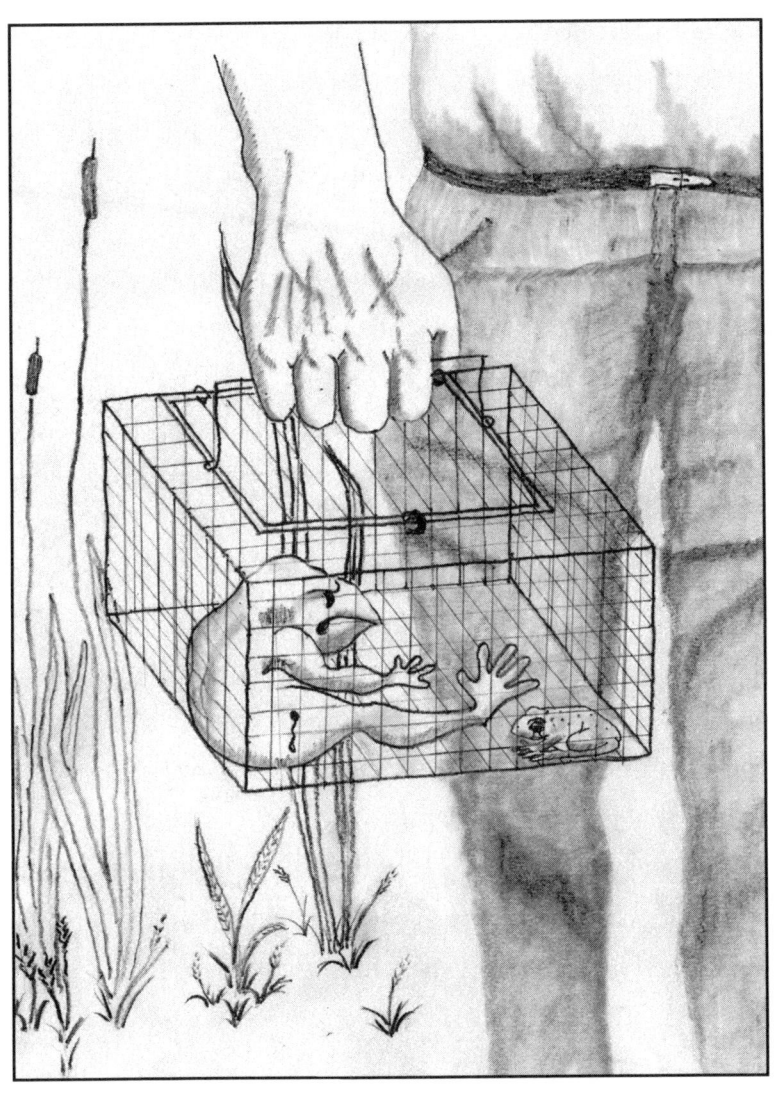

The human had suddenly returned and snatched
up the cage, carrying it away with both Sarge and me inside.

away with both Sarge and me inside.

I trembled as I tried again and again to climb to the door at the top of the cage. Each time I got near the latch, I lost my grip and fell to the bottom. It was impossible to hold on! The cage continued to swing back and forth with every step the human took.

Sarge soon became very quiet. I could see he was just as frightened as I was. His eyes began to well up with tears as he realized my attempts to free him were failing.

He slowly turned and looked me in the eye. "Save yourself, little frog," he cried softly, "and know that I will never forget your kindness. It has been a long time since anyone has been this kind to me. Now go, while you have the chance! Jump, before it is too late."

It was hard to leave Sarge there, all alone and wounded. But I found myself obeying, just as I had obeyed Papa during the storm's flood.

As I turned to leap from the cage, I heard Sarge shout out, "Take care, little Frogwilla! Take care!"

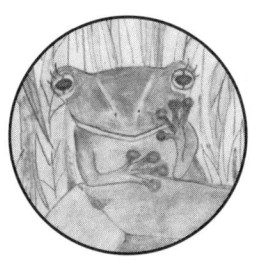

Chapter Ten
A Friend Indeed

I don't remember much after jumping from the cage. But I do remember waking up and finding myself lying upside down on some soft damp moss. And there, sitting on my chest and staring into my face, was Sunshine.

"She's alive! She's alive!" Sunshine shouted, while she gently fluttered her wings over my face. "Tucker, come quickly! Frogwilla is alive and well."

Off in the distance, I could hear the sound of something rustling through the grasses. I turned toward the sound just in time to see some kind of movement close to the ground.

"Thank goodness, you're okay!" exclaimed Tucker, as he slowly made his way through the tall swamp grass. "We were so worried about you. We spent the whole night wandering around the swamp looking for you. If it wasn't for our new friend, we would never have found you."

As I started to roll myself over, I noticed a familiar figure standing right behind Tucker . . . it was Sarge.

I tried rubbing my eyes, thinking I would surely awaken to find that I was only dreaming. But when I opened my eyes, there he was, just as big as ever.

"Why . . . I mean . . . how did you ever escape from the humans?" I asked, still thinking this must be a dream.

Sarge gave a large grin as he explained how I had, unknowingly, managed to loosen the latch on the door of the cage before jumping to my freedom. Sarge went on to explain that when the human finally set the cage down he was able to push open the door and quickly hop away. Then, as he was making his way back to the swamp, he found Tucker and Sunshine wandering around in the dark, lost and looking for me. Together, they continued searching the swamp until they found me lying on the moss.

"I must go now," said Sarge, as he looked up at the sun sinking low in the sky. "It won't be long before the humans return to hunt once again. But before I leave, I will tell you how to get to Mount Mole Hill."

Sarge could tell by the look on my face that I was surprised he mentioned Mount Mole Hill.

"You see, Frogwilla," Sarge began, "last night Tucker and Sunshine told me all about the flood that separated you from your mama and papa and about your journey to find them. They said you heard that someone who lives in Mount Mole Hill might be able to help you. Is that right?"

I sat there in a daze. I couldn't believe what I was hearing. Sarge not only knew about Mount

Mole Hill, but he also knew how to get there.

"Mount Mole Hill," I quickly answered. "Yes! Yes! That's right. And do you know who that someone might be?"

I watched as Sarge picked up one of his very large front toes and pointed in the direction of the setting sun. "Go this way, my friends," he said. "Once you leave the swamp, you will come to a lush green meadow filled with beautiful flowers. And there, just beyond the meadow, you will find many hills of freshly dug dirt. That, my friends, is Mount Mole Hill. And the someone you are looking for is a mole who goes by the name of Mr. Burrows. I am certain that if there is anyone who can help you find your parents, it is he. That mole knows something about everything and everyone who has ever come through these parts. It is said that he has a nose for news! Now I must leave you to your travels. Go carefully, little ones."

We thanked Sarge for all he had done and especially for his kindness.

As we said our goodbyes, we promised to someday meet again.

Part Three
Small Acts of Courage

Chapter Eleven
Mr. Burrows

By the time we made it out of the swamp, it was dark. After pushing our way through some thick underbrush, we decided to bed down for the night. Everyone needed a good night's rest.

I awoke the next morning feeling damp. I lifted my head just in time to feel a drop of water fall from a leaf and gently land on my nose. It had rained while I slept.

This was the first time since the storm that I had felt the rain on my skin. But this time it was different, the raindrop felt warm and soft . . . nothing like the hard-pounding rain before the flood.

I turned to see Tucker just coming out of his shell to greet the morning. He slowly lifted up his head and began to wander over my way. "Has it been raining all night? Where's Sunshine?"

"I'm not sure," I replied. "I haven't been awake for very long. But now that you ask, I haven't seen nor heard her this morning."

Before we knew what was happening, Sunshine greeted us, as usual, with one of her circle fly-overs. "Good morning, sleepyheads. While the two of you were resting your eyes, I flew off and scouted the area. I think I may have found the meadow Sarge was talking about."

That got our attention. Both Tucker and I were now wide awake.

"And Mount Mole Hill?" I quickly asked. "Beyond the meadow, did you see anything that looked like dirt hills?"

Sunshine paused for a moment and then began fluttering around with excitement. "I was saving that bit of news for a surprise. You see, while I was out scouting the area, I found this narrow dirt path. I flew as close to the ground as possible, trying hard not to lose sight of the path. Then, just as the path ended — there it was, just as Sarge described, a land full of lots and lots of dirt hills. I'm sure it must be Mount Mole Hill!"

We looked at one another, excited and nervous at the same time. My heart began to beat faster and faster just thinking about the possibility of finding Mama and Papa.

With our spirits high, we headed for the path, Mount Mole Hill and Mr. Burrows.

The walk through the meadow took longer than expected. Tucker took great delight in stopping now and then to nibble on some meadow strawberries. Sunshine amused herself by racing other dragonflies she met along the way. Meanwhile, I spent my time watching out for snakes, skunks, and others that might find me a tasty treat. We only rested for a short time, just long enough to take some sips from a puddle left over from the night's rain.

Traveling over the narrow path, I could see the meadow begin to thin out, just as Sarge had predicted. Then, off in the distance, I saw what appeared to be many large hills made of dirt and gravel. And there, in the middle of these mounds of dirt, sat the largest hill of all.

My curiosity got the best of me. Slowly, but carefully, I approached the large hill. Soon I heard a strange little voice coming from deep inside.

As I moved closer to get a better look, an odd looking creature emerged from beneath a cloud of dust. It was a furry creature, about the size of a large mouse. It had short, dark hair and huge, flat feet with large, sharp claws. Its nose was long and pointy, nothing like a mouse's. But the oddest thing of all was that it had these two round, see-through circles resting right on top of its nose . . . just in front of its two tiny eyes.

"Why, hello there," announced the furry creature, a bit startled. "What can I do for you? As you can plainly see, I am quite busy working on a new tunnel. I used to have hundreds, you know!"

Gathering my thoughts, I cleared my throat before speaking. "My friends and I are looking for a mole named Mr. Burrows. We were told he lives in Mount Mole Hill. Would you happen to know where we might find him?"

I watched the mouse-like creature wiggle and squirm its way out from the clutches of the dirt hole before finally speaking. "Why, my dear little frog, you *are* in Mount Mole Hill. And you *are* speaking to him. *I* am Mr. Burrows. How may I help you?"

Not sure what to say, Sunshine and Tucker looked my way and nodded their heads. I could see it was now going to be up to me to do all the talking.

I tried my best to keep my story short. Beginning with the flood that separated me from Mama and Papa and ending with Sarge telling me how Mr. Burrows could help me find my parents.

"It is true," Mr. Burrows began, as he adjusted

I watched the mouse-like creature wiggle and squirm its way out from the clutches of the dirt hole before finally speaking.

the see-through circles on his nose, "I do know quite a lot. I hear everything when I travel inside my tunnels . . . I miss nothing! I once had miles and miles of underground tunnels. But the flood waters came and washed them out. Now, as you can plainly see, I am doing my best to dig new ones as fast as I possibly can."

"Do you think you might have heard something about my mama and papa?" I impatiently asked.

Before Mr. Burrows could answer, Tucker spoke. He told Mr. Burrows that he thought he had seen my parents shortly after the flood, floating together on a broken branch, drifting down the flood water. And then what Tucker said next got Mr. Burrows' attention. Tucker told him about my mama's trill, her special way of singing.

"Yes! Yes!" Mr. Burrows exclaimed. "Now I remember! I did hear something about a pair of treefrogs that were looking for their offspring after the flood. One of the treefrogs was said to make a unique sound. The sound was beautiful, like a bird singing."

"That's my mama!" I yelled. "I just know it!"

I was so excited, I couldn't control myself. I leaped for joy, almost landing on Tucker's head. "Can you tell me where they might be?"

I watched as Mr. Burrows' face slowly filled with great sadness. "Well, I don't wish to be the one to tell you this, little frog. But I heard the treefrogs were captured by humans and are now being held as prisoners inside their camp."

His words sent a cold shiver down my back.

Captured! Humans! Prisoners!

Chapter Twelve
The Road of No Return

I do not know how long I stood before Mr. Burrows in complete silence. But at that moment, my thoughts were only on Mama and Papa and Mr. Burrows' words . . . *captured, humans, prisoners!*

"There, there, my little one," said Mr. Burrows, as he wiped some dirt from his see-through circles. "That was the bad news. The good news is you are very close to where the humans live. Their camp lies straight ahead, just beyond the long fence that guards the giant trees."

As Mr. Burrows continued to clean off his

circles, he told us more about his miles and miles of underground tunnels. He said that some of his tunnels actually led right up into the middle of the human camp. But, unfortunately, the flood waters had destroyed them too and he hadn't found enough time to dig new ones.

"It is a bit more difficult to tunnel under the thick stone road that separates Mount Mole Hill from the human camp," he began to explain. "It is a very long and wide road, made just for humans, by humans. The dirt is much harder to dig through — nothing like the dirt under Mount Mole Hill."

"What kind of a road is this stone road?" I asked.

Mr. Burrows scratched his head while he mumbled something about there being no safe passage. Then he paused for a brief moment and began to tell us more about this road — he called it the Road of No Return.

"You see, little frog, humans use it to travel from one place to another. They ride inside these big, noisy, smelly machines called carriers. These carriers can easily outrun anything that lives around here. Many creatures, young and old, large and small, have tried to cross the road. Some have made it safely to the other side. Others have had the misfortune of losing an arm or a leg, or worse yet . . . their lives."

As I watched and listened to Mr. Burrows, my thoughts instantly returned to Mama and Papa. *Please, please, let the treefrogs Mr. Burrows heard about be my mama and papa. And if they are, please let them be okay!*

Then, without saying another word, Mr. Burrows quickly turned and disappeared inside his newly dug hole.

I turned around to see Sunshine and Tucker quietly talking among themselves. As I approached them, I overheard the words, "Road of No Return." I was certain they were questioning if they should continue with me on my journey.

I watched my two friends as they turned to face me. Sunshine was the first to speak.

"Frogwilla," Sunshine began, "from the first

time we met, I saw how much you loved and missed your mama and papa. You have never given up searching for them. I never knew my parents. But if I had, I too would do whatever I needed to do to find them. You are the bravest little treefrog I know. No human road is going to stop us now! Together we can do this. After all, that's what friends are for!"

Tucker held his head high as he cleared his throat, then spoke. "Ditto! Or, as my father always said, 'No matter the problem, big or small, it's all for one and one for all!' Now let's go find your mama and papa!"

Then we headed for the giant trees, and the Road of No Return.

We hadn't traveled far before I heard a loud roar off in the distance. I was certain it must be a human carrier. I tried my very best not to be afraid, but to be brave. But just like climbing, it wasn't an easy thing for me to do.

It wasn't long before I saw the long fence and the

row of giant trees it guarded, just like Mr. Burrows had described.

The closer we got to the trees the louder the roar became and the faster my heart pounded.

Sunshine began to hover closer to the ground, close to Tucker, with me leading the way. Quietly, and with great care, I crept over some moss that grew near the trunk of one of the giant trees. Then slowly I inched my way around the far side of the tree. That's when I saw it, the Road of No Return.

It was the only human-made road I had ever seen. There seemed to be no beginning, no end to this road. It stretched far beyond the two long rows of giant trees, disappearing beneath the sky. The trees stood straight and tall, their top leafy branches reaching out over the middle of the road, almost touching the branches of the trees on the other side.

As I slowly made my way to the edge of the road, I saw what looked like a small squirrel lying on the other side. It appeared to be sleeping. It didn't take me long to realize it was not asleep. I was

Suddenly, I saw this huge box-like thing zoom past me.

certain it had become a victim of a carrier.

Suddenly, I saw this huge box-like thing zoom past me. It raced by so fast I couldn't see much of anything. But its noise and smell soon led me to believe I had just seen my first human carrier. As I watched it drive out of sight, I began to wonder if any one of us would ever make our way to the other side of this human-made road.

"Frogwilla, get away from the road!" Tucker yelled, as he slowly wandered out from behind the tree. "Do you want to lose a leg or something?"

"Tucker is right," Sunshine said. "Everyone stay put. I will do what I do best. I will scout the area and look for the human camp. After all, I believe I am the only one who can make it safely to the other side of this Road of No Return."

Tucker and I knew, without a doubt, that Sunshine was right. So we nodded our heads and agreed to stay put and wait for her to return, hopefully with good news.

Together we sat beneath the tree and watched as the sun slowly began to set behind the row of giant trees that lined the opposite side of the road. We waited and waited and waited. Then darkness fell. Still there was no sign of Sunshine.

Chapter Thirteen
One Courageous Leap

The next thing I remember hearing was Sunshine's voice.

"Wake up! Wake up, Frogwilla!"

Startled, I jumped up to see Sunshine, safe and sound, hovering right above me. It was only then that I realized I had slept through the night.

"I have great news," Sunshine said, proudly grinning from ear to ear. "Not only did I find the human camp, but I think I may have found your mama and papa!"

I couldn't believe what I had just heard. This

was the news I had hoped for!

"Tucker! Tucker, did you hear that?" I shouted, leaping for joy.

Tucker was already awake and munching on some tender young ferns. He had been so interested in his breakfast that he hadn't heard Sunshine return with her exciting news.

I had so many questions for Sunshine. I didn't know where to begin. *Was she sure it was Mama and Papa? Were they hurt? Were they really prisoners?*

As Tucker turned to finally see what all the fuss was about, a carrier raced down the road, soon followed by another, then another. And then, almost as quickly as they had appeared, the carriers were gone, leaving only their horrible smell behind.

Tucker hurried as best he could and joined Sunshine and me beneath the giant tree. Together, we listened closely as Sunshine tried her best to answer my many questions.

She told us how it wasn't until dusk that she finally discovered the human camp. She had just flown over a row of flowering bushes, when suddenly she was scooped up by a net and placed inside a large see-through jar. Sunshine went on to tell us how she had tried her best to escape from the jar. But after many attempts to push off the tightly sealed lid, she became exhausted and fell to the bottom. By then it was dark. She couldn't see much of anything, only a slight shadow of something that looked like the shape of another jar sitting right beside hers. That's when Sunshine said she heard a faint, bird-like sound coming from inside the other jar. But it wasn't until early morning that she saw what was inside the other jar . . . a pair of treefrogs.

Sunshine paused, taking a moment to catch her breath.

"Tell me more," I begged her. "Tell me more."

"Well, that's when the strangest thing happened," Sunshine continued. "Just as I was about to call out to the treefrogs, a human offspring opened up my jar and set me free. The offspring showed me no harm. It held the opened jar high up into the air, almost inviting me to fly away. And so I did.

"After my escape, I tried to fly back to the jar holding the treefrogs. But when I did, the offspring began waving its arms around wildly in the air. After several tries, I decided it was best to fly back to get you and Tucker."

Sunshine's story left both Tucker and me speechless. There was no doubt in my mind — the treefrogs were my mama and papa. We needed a plan to rescue them. And, to no one's surprise, Sunshine had one!

Since the Road of No Return would be quite difficult for Tucker or me to travel across safely, Sunshine had an idea . . . a solution to our problem. She explained how it might be best if Tucker would stay and wait for safe passage through one of Mr. Burrows' new underground tunnels. And how I could use my climbing skills to reach the top branches and cross the road from *above*.

I cannot begin to find the words to tell you just how frightened I was at that very moment. My toes began to sweat at the very thought of climbing up one of the giant trees. But, despite my fear, I knew Sunshine was right. Climbing seemed to be the only safe way I was going to make it to the other side. It was what I needed to do if I was going to rescue my parents. Somehow, someway, I would do my best to be brave!

It didn't take Sunshine long to find the perfect pair of trees for me to climb. Although higher than I would have liked, their branches did touch, making a beautiful arch as they hung across the road. It was as if the trees were reaching out to me — helping me to get to Mama and Papa.

And so my climb began!

Sunshine never left my side. She carefully checked out every tree branch, hovering as she guided me across each and every one. Tucker showed his support by shouting out words of encouragement from far below.

To my surprise, I made my way to the top of the tree in good time and without much difficulty. I simply took it one step at a time, hugging each branch, as I cautiously made my way high above the road.

I was just about to leap toward a branch on the other side, when I felt my toes begin to lose their grip. I quickly looked down to see the many carriers racing beneath me.

"Don't look down!" yelled Sunshine. "Frogwilla, you can do this. I know you can. Jump, Frogwilla! Jump now! You are almost across the road."

I took a deep breath and hurled myself toward the closest branch I could find. Instantly, I felt my toes and legs as they firmly grabbed hold of a large branch. *Yes! Yes! I had made it across the Road of No Return.* I was so proud of myself! Suddenly there was a loud snap! I soon felt myself falling. Down, down, down I fell. Without stopping to think, I sprang from the falling branch. Then, with a loud thud, I landed on the ground. As I turned around, I saw an old, dead tree limb lying close by. I hopped right over and began to climb up for a better look around.

That's when I saw them. There, no more than a few frog-lengths away, were a pair of humans.

It was too late to leap for cover.
So I lay perfectly still, clinging to the dead limb.

It was too late to leap for cover. So I lay perfectly still, clinging to the dead limb. I silently watched as the two humans, one much smaller than the other, walked toward me. Closer and closer they came, until they were standing directly in front of the limb, and me. That's when I noticed something dangling from the arm of the smaller human. It was something I had seen before. It was a *net*.

Chapter Fourteen
The Human Camp

Up until that moment, the only time I had seen a human's net was back at the swamp. I had not forgotten how that ended. I did not want to become a prisoner, but I feared it was too late. I could only hope the humans had not noticed me lying on the dead limb.

I cannot explain what happened next. I only know that it did. As I watched and waited, the most incredible thing happened: The smaller human put down the net. It set the net on the ground, bent down, and gently lifted me up with its hands. The next thing I knew, I was staring into the face of a young human offspring.

I was so frightened. I sat trembling as the offspring nestled me in the palm of its hand. Somehow it knew I was afraid. With a gentle touch, the offspring began to softly stroke my back. And as it did, it sang. Its voice was soft and pleasant to my ears. This human was not like the ones in the swamp. It was different. It was friendly and kind. Suddenly I was unafraid.

It wasn't very long before the human offspring returned me to where it had found me. I watched as it joined the other human and turned and walked away. As I lay there on the limb, I secretly wished I knew how to speak to humans. Then maybe, just maybe, I could have asked them about my mama and papa.

While I watched the pair of humans slowly disappear into the meadow grasses, I heard something whizz over my head. It was Sunshine. So much had happened since I last saw Sunshine;

I hadn't even noticed she was missing.

"Frogwilla, I have been looking all over for you," said Sunshine, as she darted back and forth in front of me. "I lost sight of you once you landed on the other side of the road. If I had known you were going to change colors on me, I might have found you sooner."

I had no idea what Sunshine was talking about until I looked down at my front legs. It was then I noticed something about me was quite different: I was no longer green. I was now gray — the same color as the dead tree limb I was resting on. As I sat there staring at myself, I could hear my papa's words, *"Someday, Frogwilla, you will be able to change colors, just like me."* This was my *someday*. Papa would be proud!

After spending a few moments admiring my new look, I told Sunshine about my encounter with the humans. Sunshine smiled and said she wondered if it might not be the same human offspring that set her free from the jar.

We agreed that anything was possible.

"Now that I've found you," said Sunshine, "we must move quickly, before the humans return to their camp. If you follow me, I can take you to where I last saw the jar with your mama and papa inside."

It was now high noon. As we approached the human camp, Sunshine insisted I hide among the flowering bushes that bordered the camp. Sunshine explained that once she was sure it was safe, she would return for me. Then together we would find a way to rescue my parents.

As I patiently waited inside the bushes, I saw the human camp for the first time. It was filled with these gigantic box-like homes — nothing like my comfy, cool nest in Willow's End. Each home looked the same except for being covered in different colors. The grasses that covered their camp grounds were much thicker and greener than the meadow grasses I was used to. I was certain it would be easy to leap through — easy for me to get to Mama and Papa.

I soon heard the familiar sound of Sunshine's

wings as she returned to my safe hiding place in the bushes. "We must move now," said Sunshine. "The human camp is unguarded. Your mama and papa are still inside the jar. Hurry, Frogwilla! You must leap faster than you have ever leaped before."

I quickly remembered how hard it was to keep up with Sunshine. She was amazingly fast. Each time I jumped high into the air, she would pause and hover for a moment. I could see her wings glitter in the sunlight. I knew Sunshine was doing everything she could to make it easy for me to follow her.

Then suddenly, I saw Sunshine land on top of a see-through jar sitting high atop a wooden table. And there, inside the jar, were a pair of treefrogs.

Before I reached the table, Mama began to call out my name with her special trill. Then Papa joined in; it was music to my ears.

"Is that you, my little Frogwilla?" Mama and Papa cried out with joy. "Is it really you?"

"Yes, Mama! Yes, Papa! It's really me," I answered, as I leaped and climbed high onto the

And there, inside the jar, were a pair of treefrogs.

wooden table. "My friend Sunshine and I are here to set you free. Soon we will be together again. Just like you said, Mama!"

As I pushed my nose up to the jar, I could see that something was wrapped around one of Papa's front legs. He slowly moved toward me, rubbing his nose against the inside. The only thing now separating us from each other was the wall of the see-through jar.

Sunshine and I tried our best to push the jar back and forth. We were certain that if we could get the jar rocking, it would topple over, loosening the lid just enough to fall off. But even with Mama and Papa pushing from the inside, the jar would not budge. We soon realized this was going to be more difficult than either Sunshine or I had expected. We needed to do something, and we needed to do it now — before the humans returned.

Chapter Fifteen
The Rescue

I could feel my muscles growing tired as I tried my very best to help push the jar over. We all tried our best, even Papa with his bandaged leg. As I turned toward Sunshine, I could see that she, too, was exhausted from her efforts. Her glimmering wings now lay limp and spread out beside her. But it wasn't long before I realized something else was wrong. With her head hung low, I watched as Sunshine struggled to lift her body up into the air. But, alas, she could not. As I moved closer, I discovered that one of Sunshine's wings was now lying beneath her body.

"I'm sorry, Frogwilla," said Sunshine, as she tried again and again to fly. "I can't help you rescue your mama and papa. I think one of my wings is broken."

As much as it saddened me to leave Sunshine, I knew what had to be done. If anyone was going to rescue my mama and papa it had to be me, and it had to be now!

I watched as Mama, once again, tried to crawl up the inside of the jar, hoping to loosen the lid. Only to slide down to the bottom, like before.

"If only I were a bit bigger," I cried out to Mama and Papa. "Then maybe I could make this jar topple over and you both would be free!"

Slowly, Mama made her way to my side of the jar. She gently laid her nose against the jar's see-through wall that separated us. Then, in her special trill, she began to sing. "Remember, Frogwilla, it's not about how others see you on the outside, it's how you see yourself on the inside that matters. It takes courage to believe in yourself."

I knew Mama was right. Even though I was afraid of failing, I had to try. I was not going to let this jar defeat me.

So I puffed out my chest and stood as tall as my legs would allow.

"I won't give up!" I said, bravely. Then I took a deep breath and placed my legs up against the jar. Every muscle I had was about to be put to the test.

Just as I was about to give my strongest push ever, I felt something land on the table with a crashing thud, soon followed by an all-too-familiar bellow. It was Sarge!

"Why, hello there, my young friend," Sarge said, as he looked toward the jar holding my parents. "Tucker said you and Sunshine might need a little help."

I slowly nodded my head as I looked back at Sunshine. Then I turned and looked back at the jar. There was no need to explain. Sarge seemed to understand what needed to be done.

Without saying another word, Sarge bent down, looked me straight in the eye and said, "Then let's do this together. Let's free your mama and papa."

Before I could blink an eye, Sarge huffed and puffed, and with one long leap, used his huge, strong legs to help me push over the see-through jar.

"You did it!" shouted Sunshine. "You and Sarge . . ."

But before Sunshine could finish, the unexpected happened: The jar began to roll! We all watched helplessly as the fallen jar headed toward the edge of the table, with Mama and Papa still inside. It rolled over and over until it finally rolled right off the table and landed on the ground. Quickly, I leaped straight to the ground.

As soon as I reached the jar, I saw that the lid had somehow fallen off. And there, beside the lid, sat my mama and papa. Finally, they were FREE!

"Mama! Papa!" I cried out with joy. And with one giant leap, we were together again — Mama, Papa, and me. It was the happiest moment of my life.

But just as Mama was giving me one of her

And with one giant leap, we were together again —
Mama, Papa, and me.

loving nose rubs, I heard the roar of a human carrier. With all the excitement, I had forgotten we were still inside the human camp. We needed to leave. The humans had returned.

"Follow me," Sarge ordered, as he led the way through the bushes that bordered the camp. "Tucker and Mr. Burrows are waiting with a new tunnel to give you safe passage under the Road of No Return."

And so we all followed. But after only a short distance Sarge could see that both Papa and Sunshine were having a hard time keeping up. Then to my surprise, Sarge leaned down and invited us all to climb onto his back. He said it would make traveling much faster and easier on Papa's leg, and Sunshine's wing.

After carefully thinking it over, Papa agreed.

It was the most amazing ride! It was like we were all getting a froggy-back ride. Only this time we called it a *bully-back* ride. I had never jumped so high or so far with one leap, as I did that day. Everyone was impressed, even Sunshine.

Thanks to Sarge, we managed to reach the road just as the sun was touching the lower branches of the giant trees. And there, patiently waiting for us with a new tunnel were Mr. Burrows and Tucker. It was a sight to behold.

Mr. Burrows quickly took charge as he proudly escorted everyone into his tunnel – Mama and Papa first, followed by me, then Sunshine and Tucker.

Sarge patiently waited until we were all safely inside the tunnel before leaving to rejoin his army of bullfrogs. Once again, we said our goodbyes. But this time there were no promises to meet again.

As we traveled through the large tunnel, Papa began to tell us about their journey to find me. He told us how the rapidly flowing flood waters had taken him and Mama far, far, away . . . into places they had never been before. It was many days before they could begin to search for me. They searched near and far, high and low. But their journey suddenly ended when Papa injured his leg as he tried to cross a large stone road. You see, that's when a young human offspring found my parents and gently placed them inside a jar to care for them while Papa's leg mended.

Sunshine and I looked at each other and smiled. Somehow we knew how Papa's story was going to end.

And here, my friend, is where my story ends. But remember . . . where one story ends, another begins.

The real Frogwilla.

A Note From the Author

My grandchildren have always played a big role in my passion for writing and publishing children's picture books. But when one of my granddaughters, Hannah, asked if I might consider trying my hand at writing a chapter book, I wasn't quite sure if I had the talent for jumping into another genre. Loving a challenge, it didn't take long for me to decide to give it a whirl, especially after falling in love with Hannah's e-mail address. You see, when Hannah's mother allowed her to have her first e-mail account, she chose to use the name, Frogwilla. And Hannah loves frogs . . . anything and everything to do with frogs! As luck would have it, my husband and I had a treefrog that loved to visit our flower garden and hang out on our front deck during the summer. And so we named her Frogwilla. We enjoyed watching this little treefrog and listening to her sweet trill in the evenings. It wasn't long before my imagination began to take over. "I think we might have a story here, Miss Hannah!" I exclaimed. And so, *Frogwilla, A Treefrog's Story* began.

But, there's more to this story. About that same time, Hannah's sister, Aubrey, began to take an interest in art . . . not surprising to any of us since the gift of drawing runs on the Hallwood side of the family. Aubrey not only decided to take an art class in high school, but enjoyed it so much she took some private lessons as well. After seeing some of Aubrey's artwork, I had another idea. Maybe, just maybe, she might consider drawing the illustrations for my new chapter book, *Frogwilla*. Aubrey happily agreed, but only if Grandpa (my husband) would offer some guidance. *Frogwilla* was now more than a story, it was truly a family affair. This is one project I will forever hold near and dear to my heart.

Cheri

From left to right; Cheri with Granddaughters, Aubrey and Hannah Curl, and Grandpa Hallwood

Cheri L. Hallwood is the award-winning author of *Winter's First Snowflake*, *The Curious Polka-Dot Present*, and *One Wish for Winifred Witch*. She is a three-time recipient of the prestigious Mom's Choice Award and the Dove Foundation Family Seal. But first and foremost, Cheri will tell you she is the proud mother of three talented daughters and six amazing grandchildren – all girls.

Now, with the imagination and talent of two of her grandchildren and her husband, Cheri brings you her first chapter book: *Frogwilla, A Treefrog's Story*.

When not writing or spending time with her family, Cheri enjoys sharing her passion for writing by speaking with pre-school and school age children, teachers, and community organizations throughout the Midwest. She lives in Niles, Michigan with her husband, Harry.

Aubrey M. Curl is the author's second grandchild and the principal illustrator for *Frogwilla*. She is currently a senior at John Adams High School where she is in the International Baccalaureate Program and is captain of their cross country team as well as on varsity. Aubrey also participates in varsity track and has competed twice at State Level Mock Trail competitions.

When not spending time with her friends, Aubrey enjoys reading, drawing, running, and volunteering in her community. She lives in Indiana with her family.

Harry Hallwood is the author's husband and co-illustrator for *Frogwilla*. Mentored by his father, a former commercial artist, Harry loves to create artwork for his own enjoyment. Over the years he has worked with pen and ink, charcoal, pencil, watercolor, and oils. He took great pleasure in mentoring his granddaughter, Aubrey, as she worked on helping to bring Frogwilla's story to life.

Hannah P. Curl is the author's third grandchild and the inspiration for the book, *Frogwilla*. She is currently a freshman at John Adams High School. She previously attended LaSalle Academy where she was an honor roll student and played viola in the orchestra. Hannah also competed at the Indiana State Science Olympiad where she won several medals. When not spending time with her two guinea pigs, Hannah enjoys reading, golfing, and doodling. She lives in Indiana with her family.

Acknowledgments

*I am grateful to the following individuals for their
unfaltering love, patience, and support during the writing of
this young treefrog's tale: My Wonderful Family and Friends,
Karen Bachert, and Melissa Prestine.
Frogwilla and I are also greatly indebted to
Todd Neely – graphic designer and friend.
Linda Bigger – editor and friend.*